W9-CAT-709

Charlotte Zolotow
I Know a Lady

pictures by
James Stevenson

Puffin Books

PUFFIN BOOKS
Published by the Penguin Group
Penguin Books USA Inc., 375 Hudson Street, New York, New York 10014, U.S.A.
Penguin Books Ltd, 27 Wrights Lane, London W8 5TZ, England
Penguin Books Australia Ltd, Ringwood, Victoria, Australia
Penguin Books Canada Ltd, 10 Alcorn Avenue, Toronto, Ontario, Canada M4V 3B2
Penguin Books (N.Z.) Ltd, 182–190 Wairau Road, Auckland 10, New Zealand

Penguin Books Ltd, Registered Offices: Harmondsworth, Middlesex, England

First published by Greenwillow Books 1984
Published in Picture Puffins 1986
Reprinted 1987

Text copyright © Charlotte Zolotow, 1984
Illustrations copyright © James Stevenson, 1984
10 9

Manufactured in the U.S.A.

Library of Congress Cataloging in Publication Data
Zolotow, Charlotte.   I know a lady.
Summary: Sally describes a loving and lovable old lady in her neighborhood
who grows flowers, waves to children when they pass her house,
and bakes cookies for them at Christmas.
[1. Old-age—Fiction]   I. Stevenson, James, ill.   II. Title.
PZ7.Z77Iai   1986   [E]   85-43130   ISBN 0-14-050550-4 (pbk.)

Except in the United States of America, this book is sold subject to the condition
that it shall not, by way of trade or otherwise, be lent, re-sold, hired out, or
otherwise circulated without the publisher's prior consent in any form of binding
or cover other than that in which it is published and without a similar condition
including this condition being imposed on the subsequent purchaser.

TO MARGIE

On our block
there is a lady
who lives alone.

She works in her garden
and gives us daffodils in the spring,
zinnias in the summer,

chrysanthemums in the fall,
and red holly berries
when the snow falls.

She waves to us
mornings on our way to school
and smiles when we pass her house
coming home.

She invites us in to warm up
at her fire at Halloween
and gives us candy apples
she's made herself.

And at Christmas she asks us in
to see her tree
and gives us cookies
sprinkled with red and green dots.

At Easter she makes little cakes
with yellow frosting.

Sometimes we see her walking
alone
along the path in the woods
behind the houses.
She smiles at me
and knows my name is Sally.
She pats my dog
and knows her name is Matilda.

She feeds the birds
and puts cream out for the old cat
who lives across the meadow.

I wonder what she was like
when she was a little girl.
I wonder if some old lady
she knew
had a garden and cooked and smiled
and patted dogs
and fed the cats
and knew her name.

If I was an old lady
and she was a little girl
I would love her a lot
the way I do now.